THE WHITE CRANE

鶴

For
Isao and Campbell

© Illustrations Junko Morimoto 1983
© Adaptation Helen Smith 1983

First published 1983 by William Collins Pty Ltd, Sydney
First published in paperback 1985
Typeset by Savage Type Pty Ltd, Brisbane
Printed in Japan by Dai Nippon Printing Co (Hong Kong) Ltd.

National Library of Australia
Cataloguing-in-Publication data.

The white crane.

For children.
ISBN 0 7322 7355 2.

I. Morimoto, Junko. II. Title.

895.6'3'5

The White Crane

illustrated by
Junko Morimoto

Collins
Publishers
Australia

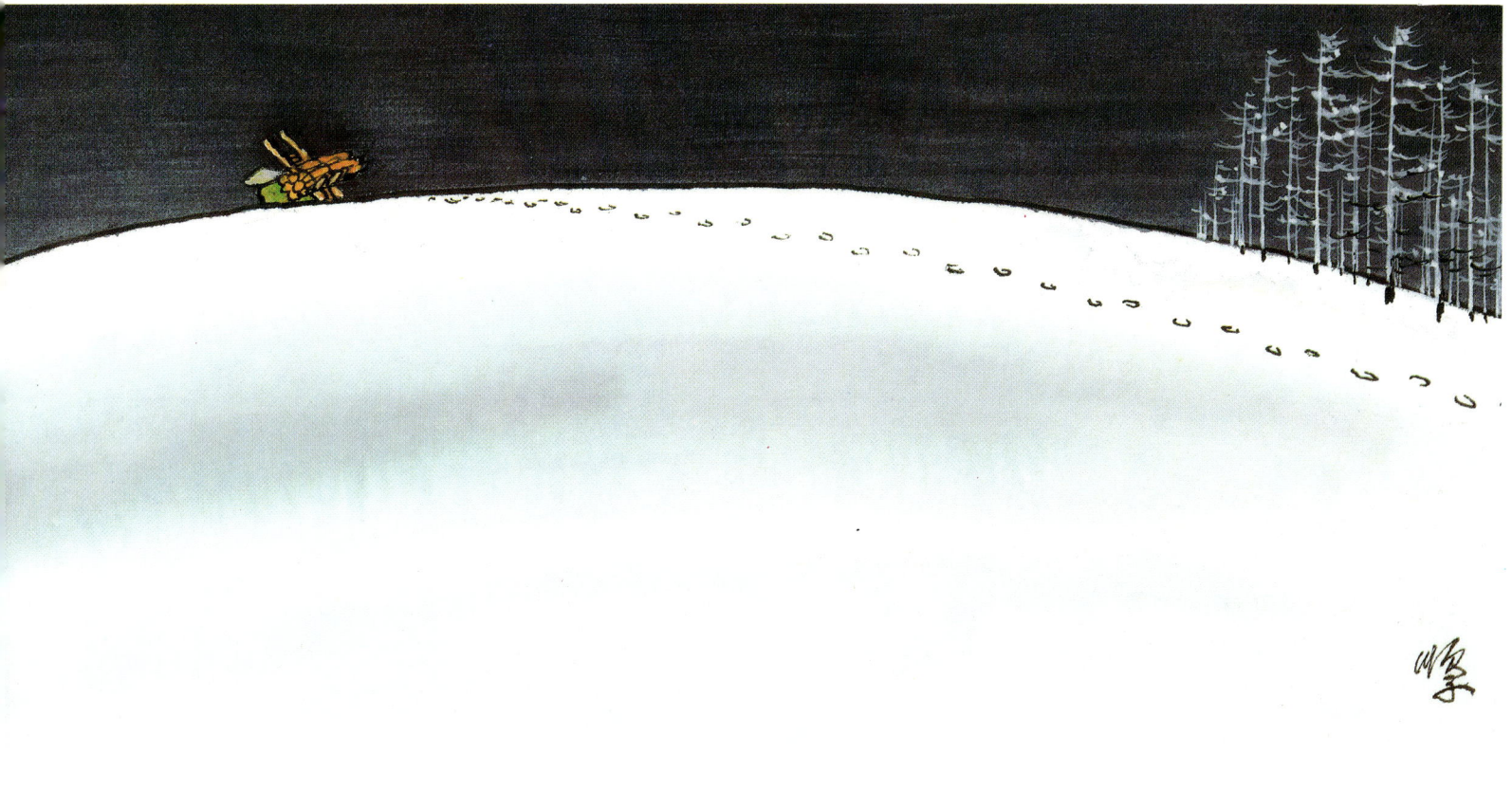

Long ago, in a remote village
in Japan, there lived
a kind-hearted old couple.
They were very poor and the old man
would go to the forest each day
to cut wood to sell
in the market.

One bitter winter's day,
the old man went into the forest,
as he always did.
The snow was thick
and the forest still and quiet.
He began to chop the wood.
Suddenly, through the icy silence,
he thought he heard a strange sound.
Yes, there it was again,
a small voice calling . . . calling . . .
"Please, help me . . . help me . . ."

Step by step
the old man struggled through the snow,
towards the sound.
There in front of him
lay a beautiful white crane,
its wings shining in the snow.
In a melancholy voice it sang,
"Oh, please old gentleman,
my leg is caught,
please will you help me?"
He hastened towards it.
"How could this have happened?
Hold still now while I help you."
With a swift and gentle movement
the old man freed the white crane.
"You have your freedom
once more beautiful crane,
take care and return safely home."

That evening,
in the warmth of their cottage,
the old couple were enjoying
their meagre meal
and discussing the day's happening.
Suddenly,
there was a knocking at the door.
"Who could be out
on such a miserable night?"
the old woman wondered.
She opened the door, and there,
standing in the snow,
was a beautiful young girl.
Jet black hair
framed her delicate face.

"Come in, come in, you poor girl!"
the old woman exclaimed.
"Quickly, over by the fire
and warm yourself.
You are as cold as ice."
"Who are you, my dear?
Where are your parents
to leave you on such a night ?"
inquired the old man.
Bowing her head
the young girl spoke very softly,
"I am all alone.
I have no parents, no name . . ."
"Then you must stay with us.
We too, are alone and would love
to have you as our daughter.
Your beauty and grace remind me
of the white crane I met today,
so we will call you Otsuru after it."

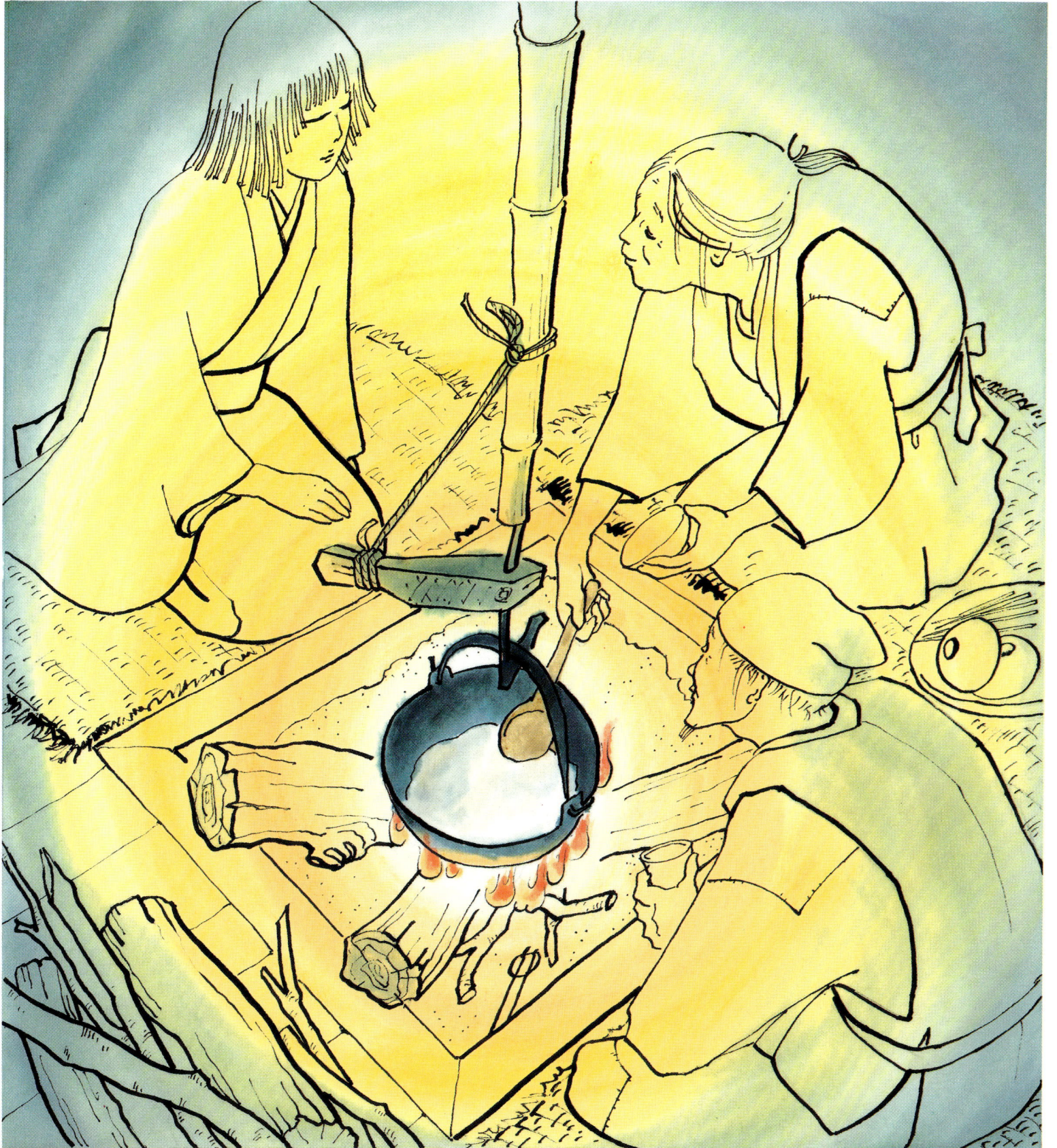

The days passed and this small family
lived very happily.
Otsuru brought laughter and joy
to the old couple, who loved to watch her
singing and dancing
with the village children.

However, times were hard
and the winter was proving long
and severe.
It saddened Otsuru
to see her father go out each day
into the icy forest to chop wood.

One day Otsuru asked to be allowed
to weave some cloth.
Going into the small room
Otsuru turned to the old couple,
"Please do not enter
until I am quite finished,"
she requested.
Patiently the old couple waited.
They could hear the shaft of the loom
as it moved swiftly to and fro.
It seemed as though
Otsuru would never stop.

At last, late into the night,
the hum ceased and Otsuru emerged.
In her arms she held
the most exquisite silk cloth.
It was as soft as down
and the colours
were nature's most delicate.
"But how did you weave such cloth?"
the old couple asked
over and over again.
"Please, my parents,
do not ask me to explain.
I must not tell you.
You can sell this cloth
and then we will have money to last us
through this terrible winter.
Father, no longer will you have to go
out into the snow."

The next day
they carefully wrapped the cloth
and, placing it on his shoulders,
the old man set off
to the silk merchant's shop.

On seeing the beautiful silk
the merchant offered him a pile of gold.
In fact, more gold than the old man
had ever imagined.

That night the old couple thanked Otsuru
and praised her many times.
It was hard for them to believe
that for the first time in their lives,
they had an abundance of food.
Of course, this made Otsuru very happy.
She loved the old couple dearly
and their little cottage
had become her home.

Many months later
Otsuru went to the old couple.
"I will go once more
into the weaving room.
You must promise not to look inside
while I work."
She spoke solemnly
and the old couple silently nodded.
Days passed.
Whoosh . . . whoosh . . .
the loom hummed.
Still Otsuru did not appear.
The sound never ceased for a moment.
At last the old woman
could stand it no longer,
"I must look, just briefly,
to see if Otsuru is alright."
Silently she slid open the door . . .
just a fraction . . .
holding her breath she peeped inside . . .

"Oh, no!" she gasped
and fell back.
"I don't understand.
How can it be?"
Inside
Otsuru was nowhere to be seen.
A magnificent white crane
stood there.
With each shift of the loom
it pulled a feather
from its wing
and wove it into the cloth.
Hearing the gasps
the crane turned and moved
gracefully from the loom.
As the old couple watched
the white crane disappeared
and in its place stood Otsuru.

"Oh my dearest parents,
I begged you not to enter!"
Otsuru lowered her head and wept.
"Now that you know my true form
I cannot remain."
Through her tears Otsuru explained,
"I am the crane which you rescued
from the snow.
I came to repay you
for giving me my life."
"Forgive us!" the old couple cried.
"Please stay with us,
we love you dearly. Please . . ."
they pleaded.

"I cannot."
Otsuru's voice was just a whisper.
As they watched
Otsuru faded and there stood
the magnificent white crane again.
Slowly, it spread its wings,
tears glistened in its eyes.
In a moment it was gone.
All that could be heard
was the moaning of the wind
and a small voice calling . . .
"Mother, Father, do not forget me . . ."